THIS IS ME!

2022

RAPT BY RHYME

Edited By Andrew Porter

First published in Great Britain in 2022 by:

Young Writers
Remus House
Coltsfoot Drive
Peterborough
PE2 9BF
Telephone: 01733 890066
Website: www.youngwriters.co.uk

Printed and bound in the UK by BookPrintingUK
Website: www.bookprintinguk.com
YB0505Q

FOREWORD

For Young Writers' latest competition This Is Me,
we asked primary school pupils to look inside
themselves, to think about what makes them unique,
and then write a poem about it! They rose to the
challenge magnificently and the result is this fantastic
collection of poems in a variety of poetic styles.

Here at Young Writers our aim is to encourage creativity
in children and to inspire a love of the written word, so
it's great to get such an amazing response, with some
absolutely fantastic poems. It's important for children to
focus on and celebrate themselves and this competition
allowed them to write freely and honestly, celebrating
what makes them great, expressing their hopes and
fears, or simply writing about their favourite things.
This Is Me gave them the power of words. The result
is a collection of inspirational and moving poems that
also showcase their creativity and writing ability.

I'd like to congratulate all the young poets
in this anthology, I hope this inspires them
to continue with their creative writing.

CONTENTS

Green Lane Primary & Nursery School, Worcester Park

Bella Helena Freeze (11)	65
Ronnie Swann (10)	66
Liliana Rawlence (10)	67
Millie Akerman (10)	68
Daniel McGuigan (8)	69
Felix Walker (8)	70
Freya Beaton (10)	71
Alice Gilbody (10)	72
Isabella Carro (10)	73
Harry Falck (11)	74
Chloe Lush (10)	75
Teagan Cox (11)	76
Chloe Fourie (7)	77
Jake Scott (9)	78

Old Hutton CE Primary School, Old Hutton

Hattie Partington (11)	79
Jacob Cowan (11)	80
Jasmine Bateman (11)	83
Ava Sophia Natlacen (10)	84
Florence Bateman (11)	86
Eleanor Daisy Wilkinson (10)	88
Tyson Bri Harvey (10)	90
Jake Berry (11)	91
Owen Gravell (11)	92
Ethan Mansfield (10)	93
Elliott Oliver Natlacen (10)	94
Lucas Robinson (11)	95

Temple Learning Academy, Halton Moor

Shakar Hassan (10)	96
Avie King (9)	97
Harper-Leigh Ellis (9)	98
Nevaeh De Groot (10)	99
Alana Fleming (9)	100
Edward Dean (9)	101
Seb Walker (9)	102

Erikson Camara (9)	103
Shelley Wood (8)	104
Marcel Dean (8)	105
Thomas Paul Hopkins (8)	106
Scarlett Burgess-Hall (7)	107
Harry Keeligan-Wright (8)	108
Emelia Barton (8)	109
Lois Gyimah (8)	110
Maison Brady (8)	111
Lobopo Nkala (8)	112
Sylvia Golonka (8)	113
Joel Spenceley (7)	114

The Pilgrim School, Borstal

Tilly Jones (9)	115
Daniel Wang (9)	116
Archie Haviland (9)	118
Honami Ghuman (9)	120
Jasper Bassett (9)	122
Ailsa Kember (10)	124
Maggie Goodwin (7)	126
Dexter Maskell (10)	127
Alex Scrace (7)	128
Samuel Hockey (9)	129
Lacie Phillips (11)	130
Lana Moran (8)	132
Donald Bakare (10)	133
Matilda Sverha (8)	134
Harvey Bassett (9)	135
Johnny Chatwell (11)	136
Jude Simmons (10)	137
Ben Friel (7)	138
Beatrice Nunn (11)	139
Isobelle Butler (10)	140
Sienna Walker (8)	141
Harshdeep Kaur (10)	142
Will Tingley (10)	143
Mabel Gisby (8)	144
Olivia Butler (8)	145
Alexander Bradley (8)	146
Alexander Swain (8)	147
Stuie Petty (9)	148
Ini Dele-Olateju (10)	149

Luca Romagnuolo (10)	150	Maxwell Libbeter (8)	192
Effie Hockley (10)	151	Ava Cave (9)	193
Isaac Thomas (8)	152	Lucy-Rose Dodson (10)	194
Nyasha Mafemera (8)	153	Freya Craig (8)	195
Amber Heydinrych (8)	154	Daisy Feltham (8)	196
Olivia Jamil (9)	155	Phoenix Collins (10)	197
Billy Cary (9)	156	Daphne Balseca (8)	198
Olivia Rayner (8)	157	Nuala Walker-Pemble (7)	199
Scarlett Moon (9)	158	Isla Thomas (8)	200
Tommy Martin (7)	159	Finlay Ashby (7)	201
Mason Kelly (9)	160	Beau Hockley (8)	202
Moses Burton (8)	161	Jack Harris (7)	203
Casey Langford (9)	162	Joshua Harrison (11)	204
Gracie Haviland (10)	163	AJ Hurkoo (9)	205
Jayden Horton-Clarke (9)	164	Logan Baxter (8)	206
Rylan Brown (9)	165	Kriti Arivalakan (7)	207
Lucia Sverha (10)	166	Angel Darling (7)	208
Belle Williamson (9)	167	Koby Packman (8)	209
Nafisa Hussain (10)	168	Riley Simmons (7)	210
Felix Barker (10)	169	Joshua Sheppard (9)	211
Henry Gardiner (10)	170	Olivia Lawniczak (7)	212
Mariam Miah	171		
Logan Smith (10)	172		
Jesse McDonagh (8)	173		
Charlie Horan (8)	174		
Shontelle Gonzalo-Apolinario (10)	175		
Hollie Atkins (8)	176		
Ini Faulkner (8)	177		
Oscar Edwards (8)	178		
Thisana Avivalakan (10)	179		
Dimitar Arabadzhiev (10)	180		
Zachary Thomas (10)	181		
Ralph Gardiner (8)	182		
Max Fuller (9)	183		
Henry Harris (9)	184		
Grace Gilbert (10)	185		
Orla Skelton (10)	186		
Ireoluwa Dele-Olateju (7)	187		
Evie Alexander (8)	188		
Riley Deards (10)	189		
Angel Eliasova (9)	190		
Bauer Packman-Fullbrook (11)	191		

THE POEMS

Get To Know Me

Up, up, up - crane your neck to catch a glimpse of my face,
As I'm the 'class giraffe' - but without the tail!
My long legs help me win the race,
I'm a hard worker - as I don't like to fail!

My dark blonde hair is neatly tied back,
White pearls are glistening from both my ears,
With my teeth brushing routine I try to stay on track,
Yet when I see a dog, I have terrible fears!

The hobbies I really enjoy: swimming, dancing, baking and art,
I write neatly and also like to read from time to time,
In acting out drama I like taking part,
My fingers are always trying to catch silly putty and slime!

Reisy Keiserman (10)
Beis Malka Girls' School, Hackney

The Strength And Weaknesses

When the world is decked in white,
Which lightens the wintery night,
There is something about this sight,
Of the snowball fight,
Throwing with all my might,
But then comes the shadows,
And put their dirty footsteps on the clean, white tablecloth,
Only leaving behind a tablecloth with dirty speckles,
I will wait until the world will once again be decked in white,
And so, this is an allegory to real life,
As we grow and fall, born so tiny and empty of sins,
But then when we do sin, we ask for forgiveness,
And change to be decked in white!

Libby Kohn (10)
Beis Malka Girls' School, Hackney

This Is Me

I'm a fast runner - my classmates all know it,
I'm fun to be around,
And I'm usually cool and calm,
My close ones say that I'm skinny,
Though I definitely weigh more than a pound
(which is 500 grams).

My favourite colour is blue though I'm picky about
shades
And I *sometimes* like pink too.

I'm very outgoing and don't mind crossing out
words
And when you read my stories,
You're in another world!

Now that I've given you some info,
You'd better buckle up and turn the page...

Dini Deutsch (11)
Beis Malka Girls' School, Hackney

Me, Myself And I

Who is 'me'?

Me is my essence
Me is my intelligence
Me is my ability to think
Me is my power
Me is my strength.

Me could have sparkly blue eyes
Me could have brown hair
Me could be short
Me could have freckles
Me could have yellow teeth.

Me could be clever
Me could be sensible
Me could be confident
Me could be a master baker
Me could be lots of fun.

All of these above are my God-given blessings
'Me' is what I do with them.

Chaya Sheindy Friedman (10)
Beis Malka Girls' School, Hackney

It's The Inside That Matters

Let me describe what you will see,
When you have a look at me.
Blue eyes and brown hair,
My skin is fair.
I'm quite tall,
But that isn't all.

Like when an apple is bruised,
And to eat it's refused.
But on the inside it really,
Tastes very dearly.

The same is with me and you,
On the outside we can look imperfect too.
But the inside if the main part,
Everything that comes from the heart.

Suri Weber (10)
Beis Malka Girls' School, Hackney

All About I

All about I,
Brown is the colour of my eye,
My voice pitch is high,
Homework makes me sigh,
But I still reach for the sky,
Because satisfaction makes me fly,
I'm not too shy,
But if I'm upset I may cry,
On my friends I rely,
I'm quite talented, I won't deny,
With song and dance, my time I occupy,
To draw and paint I really try,
My words have now run dry,
So I guess it's time to say goodbye!

Rochmy Damen (10)
Beis Malka Girls' School, Hackney

Breindy Deutsch

Being the oldest girl
In my family is the best, better than
The rest. The shining sun makes me
Cheer and the long, hot days make me
Have no fear. I just love the heat
And dance to the beat. Let me tell you
What I look like: I have my hair up
In a bun, my eyes are able in the
Sun. I'm in Year Five and I
Thank Hashem that I'm alive.
I wrote it in the shape of a
Sun, now you can go
Have fun.

Breindy Deutsch (10)
Beis Malka Girls' School, Hackney

Truly I

Based on the teaching of Jewish sages

If I am I
Because you are you
And you are you
Because I am I
Then I am not I
And you are not you
But if I am I
Because I am I
And you are you
Because you are you
Then you are truly you
And I am *truly* I!

Because I value my identity
And do not get swayed by the majority
I will not fret about popularity
And *that* is what makes me a celebrity!

Rivki Wind (10)
Beis Malka Girls' School, Hackney

Candyland

Candies I love, they're so sweet,
Each one with their own taste,
Millions, nothing can beat,
I like the toothpaste.

Candies flying all around,
Sour sticks, lollies and packets too
Long, short and also round,
Chinese, Muslim and Jews.

R eading I do when I have time,
U p, up, up until nine,
T alking, meanwhile I read,
I t helps me fall asleep.

Ruti Bard (11)
Beis Malka Girls' School, Hackney

All About Me!

Hi, my name is
Malky. I am a confident but not too
Popular girl. Something special about me
Is that I always have a
Smile. I don't smile because it's fun, I
Smile to make other people smile and be happy.
Other than that I also like playing on
A keyboard to make other
People smile and dance
With the music. I
Am clever in maths and give
Compliments.

Malky Shuvacks (11)
Beis Malka Girls' School, Hackney

Who Am I?

Twisting, twirling
One, two, three
Spinning, whirling
Gracefully
Hands up
Legs apart
The music
It's about to start
Step one
A pirouette
What fun
Like a marionette
Next is a wave
Hands moving together
Now dance towards the cave
Light as a feather
Twisting, twirling
One, two, three
Spinning, whirling
Gracefully.

Sari Sklar (11)
Beis Malka Girls' School, Hackney

Me And Myself

Hi!
My name
Is Chana Suri,
I really love maths,
It is my favourite subject,
For I know it very well,
Column addition, column subtraction and more,
I really enjoy doing art, drawing, baking, swimming,
I am a really happy, fun person,
I hope you enjoy reading it,
From the top to bottom,
I am very clever,
And very friendly,
Chana Suri
Enjoy!

Chana Suri Schweitzer (11)
Beis Malka Girls' School, Hackney

The Sum Of My Hobbies

Maths is my best
For that I wouldn't rest
Even though it's a test
I'm sure you all guessed
Additionally something I really like
Is to swing down from a ladder's high height
And to go on a long, long hike
And when I rollerblade, I fly with all my might
Here's to add
It's not bad
When friends I've had
That makes me glad.

Leile Pollock (11)
Beis Malka Girls' School, Hackney

Who Am I?

E ntering this contest, I just had to

S o let me tell you about me

T o make recipes is my dream

Y es, I like maths tests, it's funny.

A book is sure to appease me

D oing crafts in my opinion is exciting

L ittle toddlers I like to play with

E sty also enjoys writing

R eading is also my thing.

Esty Adler (9)
Beis Malka Girls' School, Hackney

Feelings

Sometimes I'm sad,
Sometimes I'm mad,
Sometimes I'm lazy,
Sometimes I'm crazy,
Sometimes I'm miserable,
Sometimes I'm flexible,
Sometimes I'm rude,
Sometimes I'm in a mood,
Sometimes I'm cross,
Sometimes I'm lost,
Sometimes I'm smiling,
Sometimes I'm shining,
But now I'm happy.

Rifka Henny Hoffman (11)
Beis Malka Girls' School, Hackney

My Hobbies

Hi
My name
Is Feigy Friedman
I have seven siblings and I am the
Third youngest and have two younger brothers
And five younger than me
My hobbies are: swimming
Dancing, singing, drawing
Baking. I'm in Year Five
With fifteen classmates
To sing is good
This is the best.

Feigy Friedman (10)
Beis Malka Girls' School, Hackney

All About Me

Hi!
My name is Liela Sprung
I go to Beis Malka School
And my favourite activity is to swim in a pool
I am very caring
And also very sharing
I really enjoy writing
I find it extremely entertaining
There is a lot more to say about me
But I think I'll have a break and drink tea.

Liela Sprung (10)
Beis Malka Girls' School, Hackney

Chayelle

C aring is my way,
H elping everyone is always okay,
A chieving and trying hard is right,
Y es with all my might,
E verything I do with a smile,
L oving to go that extra mile,
L oaded with clues to try,
E veryone to guess who am I?

Chayelle Gross (11)
Beis Malka Girls' School, Hackney

All About Me

Hi my name is Chavi, how do you do?
I have brown hair and brown eyes too
Life is fun
I have friends a ton
I like to go out to play
On a hot sunny day
I love to sing
And enjoy doodling
I have lots more to say
But I'll leave it for another day.

Chavi Weissbaum (10)
Beis Malka Girls' School, Hackney

What I Enjoy To Do!

C olouring and drawing is something I love to do,

H aving friends and neighbours over to play and chat,

A nd looking after my younger siblings makes me calm,

N othing stops me from going swimming,

I n the pool, I like to jump and swim.

Chani Grausz (10)

Beis Malka Girls' School, Hackney

At Home

At home I eat, sleep and drink
At home we have a sink
At home with my siblings I have fun
At home we each have a yummy bun
At home I have some peace
Without my nephew or my niece
Home is the best place to be
To spend time with my wonderful family!

Gitty Klein (10)
Beis Malka Girls' School, Hackney

A Limerick About Me

These are the things I love to do,
Reading, swimming, dancing and baking too.
By nature I am quite tame,
Miriam is my name,
And I am lucky to have siblings a few.

Miriam Gross (10)
Beis Malka Girls' School, Hackney

Bruchi

B ecause I am very happy I

R eally cheer everyone up.

U nderstands

C learly that

H appy

I s the most important.

Bruchi Fried (11)

Beis Malka Girls' School, Hackney

This Is Me!

My name is Leahle, you see,
I'm the youngest of the family,
Thirteen siblings above me,
I'm at the end of the family tree.

Leahle Elias
Beis Malka Girls' School, Hackney

Rivky

R uns fast

I s always happy

Lo **V** es maths

Ba **K** es a lot of

Y ummy things only.

Rivky Mandelovics (11)

Beis Malka Girls' School, Hackney

School

School
Fun, interesting
Writing, listening, looking
At the teacher when
Giving out the SATs
Paper.

Suri Zilbershlag (11)
Beis Malka Girls' School, Hackney

Anxiety

My eyes are chocolate hazelnuts
My lips sweet strawberry kisses,
My smiles warm up the coldest day,
Whispering kindness and wishes.

Waterfalls fill my eyes,
When the feelings get too large,
My lips speak brave words,
But my thoughts take charge,
I feel the world has turned its back,
My legs shiver and my lips quiver,
The thoughts of joy always come
But the poisonous messages always deliver.

But I am determined to be brave and strong,
And take the world head on,
I will never give up, I'll keep on trying,
Until these beastly thoughts are gone,
So I will keep on moving,
Even when times are tough,
I will open the door to a new world,
Where people know they are enough!

Matilda Robertson (9)
Bournemouth Collegiate Preparatory School, Parkstone

This Is Me!

Ingredients to make me.

A bit of lightning, exactly half a kilogram
Footballs, two kilograms
A bit of weirdness, one kilogram
A bit of craziness, half a kilogram
Different languages, three kilograms
Coding, one kilogram
Water, one kilogram
Games, three kilograms
A bit of intelligence, one kilogram
Travelling, two kilograms.

You need a bit of lightning
But if you add too much the frightening me will
come out.
You need a bit of coding and I'm very super
But while you make it, you have to be quiet.

You need a bit of craziness, but I'm a literal genius,
I'm the best defender in football,
I always put all into everything,
I glisten in the water but I'm also a talker.

But mostly at the end you have to say three different languages,
If you don't do all of that the recipe might go wrong and get damaged.

Last thing, I love games
And I love to travel in trains.

This is me.

Joonseo Lee (10)
Bournemouth Collegiate Preparatory School, Parkstone

This Is Me

I live in a great world
With twists and bumps but still as smooth as a
pearl
There's a game for me
To represent my personality
Puzzles are hard but I always get it right
I love making creatures, some violent, some nice
I imagine the old age where dinosaurs roamed
They're beautiful creatures and it's a shame they
had to go.

Drawing is fun, I can't say why not
It's a great experience so give it a shot
I love animals, some big, some small
But deep inside I love them all
Winter, summer, spring and autumn
Better see them
All great seasons in different places
But we haven't even scratched the surface.

I love my family and nothing else
Not one, not two but seven siblings

I'm lucky I'm not by myself
Also live in a great building
Before I was just a regular baby
But now I'm happy to call myself an Athusayni.

This is me.

Saad Athusayni (11)
Bournemouth Collegiate Preparatory School, Parkstone

Who Am I Actually?

Who am I actually?
I'm full of paints,
I have a voice,
I dance all day,
I have a choice.

I ride a bike,
I like to dream,
I like to read,
And eat some sweets,
I'm a library inside me.

Ice skate,
As the winter passes,
And in the summer,
I wear sunglasses,
And swim under the sky.

I have a pet,
His name is Raulgh,
He's so unusual,
And so clumsy,

He's as naughty,
As my brother, Alexander.

I like the nature,
And howling trees,
Some singing birds,
And gentle breeze.

I like to bake,
A big sweet cake,
With juicy berries,
And lots and lots of,
Paper fairies.

I have a family,
A kind, careful mum,
A funny dad,
And a small naughty lad,
My brother.

This is me.

Sofia Komisarovas (11)
Bournemouth Collegiate Preparatory School, Parkstone

A Bit Of Madness About Me

My twin, a villain with an evil smirk,
Why does she ruin all my work?
English and maths, they're my happy hour,
Though art and design, there I cower.
This is me.

Two birds, two fish, they're my pets,
Life is as good as it ever gets.
Minecraft, a game better than ever,
So stunning I can play forever.
This is me.

Watching Liverpool is simply heaven,
As Liverpool win nil to seven.
A million goals go flying across,
While we still haven't had a loss.
This is me.

Piano is a dream as I relax,
As I go chomp on my tasty snacks.
My friends and, running and chatting,

While also hugging and laughing.
This is me.

Smart yet funny,
Optimistic and happy.
An undergoing of trials,
As I face denials.
This is me!

Phoenebe Wu (11)

Bournemouth Collegiate Preparatory School, Parkstone

This Is Me

The coldness of the air,
Hats and gloves will be worn,
The glistening of the water,
What a sight.

My hair like the sand,
My eyes like the sea,
As you can see.

I love to sing,
Dancing too,
And my favourite colour is blue.

This is me.

Fluffy animals make me smile,
I go on for a mile,
Kind as a teacher,
Wouldn't hurt a creature.

I like to read,
Yes indeed,
Magical stories,
Give it to me!

Short as an ant,
On the hockey pitch with a stick,
That makes me click.

Off I go quick,
Speeding along,
Goal!
A strand of lightning hits the net.

Tati Richardson (11)
Bournemouth Collegiate Preparatory School, Parkstone

Things That I Do

There are a lot of things that I do like...
I love watching Marvel Studios.
My favourite is Avengers: Endgame.
I love travelling, especially Australia,
The place I really want to go is to Uluru,
It's a big mountain in the middle of Australia (the outback).
I absolutely love animals, especially dogs and hamsters!
I love playing with my dog Barnaby who is a labradorable (it probably sounds like a made-up breed).
My favourite hobby is doing epoxy resin based on anything.
My favourite food is chilli because it's really spicy and tasty.
I like chatting to friends on the iPad who are far away from home...
So that's all the things that I do.

Isadora Cooper (10)

Bournemouth Collegiate Preparatory School, Parkstone

This Is Oritsé

T his is my poem that best describes me.

H owever confident I seem, sometimes I can worry.

I ndependent, friendly and caring as can be.

S port is my passion, football my hobby.

I try to work hard in everything I do.

S choolwork, homework and helping my mum too.

O n the football pitch my heart comes alive.

R unning past defenders with the ball at my feet.

I take a shot towards the goal, hoping to score.

T he ref blows his whistle then the fans start to roar.

S inging my name from the stands is something I crave.

E very player is unique but all must be brave.

Oritsé Wilson (9)
Bournemouth Collegiate Preparatory School, Parkstone

This Is Me

Midnight hair
With a melanoid stare.
Dark as an endless void
Her obsidian eyes
Escorted with specs
That see everything...

People know
Of the mental giant.
But do they understand
The natural mastermind
An Einstein
And gifted in English.

She's the nightmare
Her rival relative.
Grasp all his secrets,
And the masked unknown.
Every single one
And every single bit.

Her mind is full
Of forever knowledge,

A library of wisdom.
A bookworm, they call her,
But none realise
The joy of reading.

Her one motto:
Be true to herself...

Dorothy Wu (11)

Bournemouth Collegiate Preparatory School, Parkstone

My Recipe

Ingredients:
Loudness, ten pounds
Chattiness, three tablespoons
Craziness, one pinch
Three bowls of pasta (any)
A room full of books
A warm bed
Smarts, 3lbs.

Take out an extra-large bowl and fill halfway up with water,
Add one pound of loudness and then add three tablespoons of chattiness and mix,
After mixing, add a warm bed and the rest of the loudness, then heat,
Once heated, add the smarts and craziness and then a room full of books,
Add hot water and mix fast until you see bubbles appear,
Whilst mixing, add the pasta and leave to heat overnight.

Noah Ostler (10)
Bournemouth Collegiate Preparatory School, Parkstone

Maldivian Girl

Born from the ashes
Of 2010.
Rose into a phoenix
And named 'Defender of Men'.
My hair long, dark and shiny.
While my eyes are big, dark and fiery!
My spirit is a wildflower.
Don't you dare try to deny me
I am brave and strong as a lion!
My screams will have you wailing just as a siren!
Born in the Pearl of India,
Surrounded by friends, buildings and heat!
My eyes are portals to different dimensions.
While my ears are secret passages leading to my mind.
Full of art, Harry Potter and Minecraft animations!
This is *me!*

Sasha Habeeb (11)
Bournemouth Collegiate Preparatory School, Parkstone

My Dreams

I have a dream...
That one day I'll be a famous tennis player
And travel across the world
To see if I can be the one to win.

I have a dream...
That one day I'll be an architect
Reaching the limits
And creating fascinating builds.

I have a dream...
That one day I'll be able to build
Anything I desire
At the reach of a hammer and nail.

I have a dream...
That one day I'll know all the secrets of space
And tell them aloud
To help push forward space travel.

Maybe I'll do it all!

Daniella Britton (11)

Bournemouth Collegiate Preparatory School, Parkstone

Me!

I am me and you are you
No one can change me
I love animals
I read books
I can ride go carts
And I can climb trees
Most people think I am quiet
But I can be loud
Not many people have heard me shout
They do know however that I love books
And my favourite animal is very quiet
A bit like me
They have a very wide smile when they are happy
I also love dogs, so cute and fluffy
My favourite movie is very new
A bit of magic is involved too
So this is me
And no one can change that.

Isabella Jeffery (11)
Bournemouth Collegiate Preparatory School, Parkstone

This Is Me

I have hair as black as night,
With eyes like chocolate opals,
I am as tall as a tower,
And as gentle as a flower.

As I grow I become kinder,
And I am a very good finder,
And am a good reminder,
As well as a minder.

I am a book reader,
An amazing leader,
A great story writer,
And a fish feeder.

I love creating,
As well as painting,
I have a good imagination,
And like to go on a vacation.

I have lots of talents,
And am very smart,
I can have a happy and sad part of me,
This is me.

Swara Mevcha (10)

Bournemouth Collegiate Preparatory School, Parkstone

My Life In Colour

If I was a colour that colour would be turquoise.
Sometimes I am blue
But most of the time I am green
And green makes me feel happy and creative.
Turquoise reminds me of the sea
Because turquoise is the sea's colour
And I see the sea every day.
When walking my puppy along the beach
It makes me feel very calm and free.
And when I go to my dad I see my rabbits
With cream, blue diamond eyes.
People think I like pink and unicorns
But I like blue and green.

Florence Newman (9)
Bournemouth Collegiate Preparatory School, Parkstone

This Is Me!

I have a pet,
A cat, a real pest.
I'm a goalkeeper,
The real best.

English, maths and science,
I'm so clever.
I have a passion for gaming,
I'll be good at it whatsoever.

I'm a bit of a shorty,
But I'm still good.
I have a brother,
But we're still in our childhood.

I like my friends,
So happy and fun.
I love my sport,
But I'm always on the long run.
This is me!

Luke Ness (10)
Bournemouth Collegiate Preparatory School, Parkstone

Larnie

I think that gymnastics
Is fantastic.
I have long hair,
But I don't care.
I get cold feet,
I can't catch the heat.
I like unicorns
With their sparkly horns.
I am super at art,
And really smart.
I am a big reader
And a cute kitten feeder.
I love words,
Nouns, adjectives and verbs!
I like looking after bugs
And I give good hugs.
So much more to say,
But my cat wants to play!

Larnie Salvatierra (8)
Bournemouth Collegiate Preparatory School, Parkstone

The Unbelievable Day

First we went to school and did a lot of stuff
Most of it was English which was actually very tough
Then we learnt a cheer
Because when we do it that's what we want to hear
Then it was break
And had a lot of cake
But suddenly something came out of nowhere
We were all very scared
Well except for me
We'll never forget that day
Especially me
'Cause it was my birthday.

Darcey Williams (10)
Bournemouth Collegiate Preparatory School, Parkstone

Me

This is the forest
Where I spend most of my time
Also a guitarist
With a rhythm that rhymes.

A love for dragons
They whoosh and roar
Lots of passions
Mixed with adventure.

My eyes are blue like ice
Or blue like the sky
They're very nice
Makeup I don't really apply.

This is the sand
This is the sea
This is the land
This is me!

Lily Edwards (10)
Bournemouth Collegiate Preparatory School, Parkstone

This Is Me

I am a friend helper,
A piano player,
A mathematician,
A cat cuddler,
Walking makes me happy,
Maths is fun too,
Choir is very exciting,
If I could be an animal I would want to be a cat,
Spicy squid legs are my favourite.

Teddy Mains (10)
Bournemouth Collegiate Preparatory School, Parkstone

Scaredy-Cat

When I wake up in the morning and there's a
spider hanging down I'd scream and shout and run
about, I really am a scaredy-cat.
I'm as scared as a mouse being chased by a cat.
If there's a small spider on the floor and I'm
walking on the carpet I'd quickly jump on the sofa
and shout out for my mum.
"Mum!"
I am as scared as a robin being chased by an
eagle!

But... if a spider's on the wall I'd suddenly become
friends with it!
I really am well-weird!

But that's not all!

I am a huge dog-lover too!
I especially like spaniels.
I have five dogs and I love them all.
Dot the dog is my favourite of course.
Olive is next,
She will jump up on my knee when I'm doing my
homework.

Frank is after that, he is so jumpy!
Ted is next, he likes to howl.
And Huey is last - he is the smart one.

Florrie Rose Bell (8)
Chirnside Primary School, Chirnside

Phoebe

P enguins. I am positive and I am a penguin-lover and I am adventurous. I am an animal lover, I am prepared and I love axolotls.

H onest. I am happy and I'm helpful. I like the colour of the clouds when the sun goes down.

O bservant. I hate oranges but I like the colour orange, I also like the colours black and blue.

E nergetic. I am excellent and I like to do gymnastics. I am elegant like a lemur and I am mischievous like a monkey.

B ouncy like a rubber ball and I am beautiful inside and out! I like

E lephants and I like emeralds, I like the colour red and I also like the colour rainbow.

Phoebe Ophelia Jacobs (8)
Chirnside Primary School, Chirnside

Me, Me, Me!

J iggly as a jelly, jolly as a jerboa.

E xtra extraordinary and fast as electricity.

S low as a sloth, small as a salamander.

S alty salami is certainly my favourite.

I nvisible pets is my favourite game, I look after baby itty-bitty baby toads.

C ute, cuddly capybara are my favourite creature.

A listair, my cousin, is never angry, and apples are his favourite fruit.

Jessica Thomson (8)
Chirnside Primary School, Chirnside

Ella-Jae

E ntertained by art.

L ove my brother Harry always. He is sometimes annoying, he loves to play with me.

L ove my pug, he is called Beau. He is so cute but sometimes he is greedy.

A nna is my friend. She is amazing as a star. We laugh all the time.

J oyful and jolly.

A rt is my favourite hobby.

E mily, Ella and Gracie are my friends.

Ella-Jae Winter Young (8)
Chirnside Primary School, Chirnside

What I'm Like!

R azor-sharp! Sometimes I am as ruthless as a raging rattlesnake but sometimes I am as soft as a red robin.

O bservant! My objective is to drink all the oval Ovaltine in this not oval world!

S agacious! I am in love with sensationally smooth sage strong tea, but I wish it was saltier!

S cottish! Snakes delight me so much, I went to sensationally hot southern Spain!

Ross Hull (8)

Chirnside Primary School, Chirnside

Alan

I am athletic at all sports
I eat apples a lot
I am amazing
I am as fast as an alligator.

I love lemurs!
I am loving life, like a leopard on a rock
Made of labradorite.

When I am an adult
I will go on an adventure all around the world.

I am nice around nature
I get nasty if people don't take care of nature.

Alan Nowak (8)
Chirnside Primary School, Chirnside

All About Me!

G reen is my least favourite colour!

R aspberries are my favourite fruit, as well as strawberries!

A lfie is my dog, I love him so much!

C old is my favourite weather, I hate heat!

I am eight years old and I am turning nine on June 23rd!

E lla-Jae, Ella and Emily are my friends, they are really funny!

Gracie Aitchison (8)

Chirnside Primary School, Chirnside

Aurora!

A m I a cat lover?

U niverse is my favourite song.

R ed is my fourth favourite colour.

O reos are my favourite biscuit.

R ain is something I don't like.

A ugust is my favourite time of the year.

Aurora Star Hall (8)

Chirnside Primary School, Chirnside

My Life

H annah is my name.

A bbey is my sister, Abbey is athletic.

N ice I am sometimes.

N ot always naughty, but sometimes!

A pples are my favourite.

H ard worker making my teacher happy.

Hannah Brown (8)

Chirnside Primary School, Chirnside

Archie

I am amazing like an alligator.
I am right-handed. I like rocks.
I am a cat lover. I am careful, I am caring.
I am happy most of the time.
I am incredible and crazy!
I sometimes wake up very early.

Archie William Donaldson (8)
Chirnside Primary School, Chirnside

Life Is Great Being Me!

M y name is Bella,

Y eah, I'm a really athletic fella.

N o, my teacher is not a woman,

A nd he doesn't support Fulham,

M y friends would call me smart but also very caring,

E llie, my sister, would probably say I'm daring.

I am eleven years old and I'm currently writing a novel,

S ome of my inspiration came from an app called Pobble

B y the way, I have a cat and a dog, the dog is Cosmo,

E veryone thinks I have a goldfish, but that was long ago,

L oving every moment is as important as loving bees,

L iving life with books is the best it can be,

A nd finally, my name is Bella and I am proud to be me!

Bella Helena Freeze (11)

Green Lane Primary & Nursery School, Worcester Park

This Is Me Ronnie

I am Ronnie, I am me, I love burger with cheese for tea,
A little ketchup with my chips and I smile as I lick my lips.
I go to school five days a week, my humour is so tongue in cheek.
My favourite lesson by far is art, and English is just off the chart.
Rugby is the best sport ever, to play you don't have to be that clever.
I have also played football too, if you haven't tried it, you should do.
My PS4 is so sick, with the controls I am so slick,
I am the best, I play online, my friends all put me to the test.
I play with my cousin Archie a lot, but sometimes he loses the plot.
I try to be kind and helpful to others and sometimes even to my brother.
This is a little about me, I must go now to have my tea!

Ronnie Swann (10)
Green Lane Primary & Nursery School, Worcester Park

Recipe For Me

First of all add the flour of adventure,
Then a sprinkle of shy baking powder,
If you want, drop in bits of musical chocolate,
The reading sugar must be added,
Pour the mixture into the mould of drawing,
Slide it into the Japanese oven,
Wait for twenty short horse-riding minutes,
After that, it should be puffy with tennis,
Squeeze the strawberry, flowery icing on top,
The space Smarties will add a melty feeling,
Finally lay the cherry of spirit and passion on top,
Now you are done and ready to stop.

Liliana Rawlence (10)
Green Lane Primary & Nursery School, Worcester Park

Millie

My name is Millie and I am a writer.
I love stories and books,
They pull me in tighter.
I hope you enjoy this poem I wrote.

A puffin is a bird not well known,
But it does what others cannot -
I think that's full blown!
And pretty awesome.

It flies, swims and walks,
And smiling at its mate,
In bird language it talks.
About what, we don't know.

Sometimes I feel just like a bird,
Just like a puffin,
When my voice is not heard
Because I am a child.

Millie Akerman (10)
Green Lane Primary & Nursery School, Worcester Park

This Is Daniel!

T alents are sports, thinking and reading,
H arry Potter is my favourite topic,
I am currently eight years old,
S chool is really fun.

I have a brother named Matthew,
S ports like football and netball are what I enjoy.

D ragon is my favourite animal,
A ugust is my birth month,
N eed to wake me up most mornings,
I magining new worlds is my hobby,
E ggs are best boiled to me,
L ack luck, I do.

Daniel McGuigan (8)

Green Lane Primary & Nursery School, Worcester Park

My Extraordinary Friday

It was raining, I was soaking, dripping wet,
But I was going to the theatre.
I, Felix, was going to be on stage.

The theatre was full of children.
I felt nervous, really nervous.
What if I did a step wrong?
What if I slipped?
Would people laugh at me?

Slowly, I stepped onto the stage.
The lights went down,
The music boomed.
The music took me out into the world,
I just danced.

Whistling, clapping, shouting
For me, Felix Walker!

Felix Walker (8)
Green Lane Primary & Nursery School, Worcester Park

My Story

My story is my cats and dog who I play with all day
and curl up with all night,
My story is the enormous oak tree that I hear the
woodpecker peck at and squirrels run up and
down,
My story is my friends and family that help me on
my journey,
My story is my home that holds all important
things that makes me feel secure and welcome,
My story is camping in the big wide woods where I
hear the birds sing and run around having fun,
My story is my chickens that cluck, cluck, cluck all
night long.

Freya Beaton (10)

Green Lane Primary & Nursery School, Worcester Park

Alice

A is for adventurous. I love climbing mountains and exploring the world.

L is for loving. I love my family and my friends and my hamster up in Heaven.

I is for inventive. I am very creative and love making songs on my piano.

C is for crazy. I am wonderfully weird and can get hyper easily.

E is for eager. I love learning new things and trying new things.

Alice Gilbody (10)

Green Lane Primary & Nursery School, Worcester Park

My Pets

My name is Isabella,
I have two dogs, a hamster, a fish, you name it,
Rocky, Crumble, Dash and Bubbles,
I wish, I wish, I wish for a rabbit,
Maybe five or seven, ten or eleven, fifteen to seventeen,
I get old, but I am ten, ten is the best,
I'm not too young, I'm not too old.
Sooner or later I might get one someday.

Isabella Carro (10)
Green Lane Primary & Nursery School, Worcester Park

Springbok

S miling as our team offload onto the pitch
P ouncing at the opposition
R unning down the touchline
I ntense gameplay
N ever giving up
G rappling at their legs
B eating each player to the ball
O ver the tryline
K icking the ball to get the conversion.

Harry Falck (11)
Green Lane Primary & Nursery School, Worcester Park

I Am Exactly Who I'm Meant To Be

I am Chloe,
From the tips of my toes,
To the top of my head,
From my brown hair,
To my ruby lips,
To my hazel eyes,
This is me.

I am sporty and love to run,
I am friendly and fun,
And I love to speedily read,
I am Chloe,
This is me,
And I am exactly who I'm meant to be!

Chloe Lush (10)
Green Lane Primary & Nursery School, Worcester Park

All Of The Things That Make Up Me

I look in the mirror
And who do I see
I see the me
I will always be
The me no one else can be.

I am proud to be me
I am glad to be me
My hair, my eyes
My personality.

My size, my shape
And the look of my face
All of the things that make up me
Inside and out.

Teagan Cox (11)
Green Lane Primary & Nursery School, Worcester Park

The Most Amazing Me

Caring Chloe thinks about other people's emotions.
Cosy Chloe curls up to read.
Creative Chloe wants to be an inventor.
Courageous Chloe seeks adventure.
Chatty Chloe has a lot to say.
Cheerful Chloe wears a smile on her face.

Chloe Fourie (7)

Green Lane Primary & Nursery School, Worcester Park

This Is Funny Me

J oyful
A lso
K ind and
E ager.

S ometimes silly
C aring of
O thers and
T hankful for
T eaching me to be me.

Jake Scott (9)
Green Lane Primary & Nursery School, Worcester Park

This Is Me!

My loving heart is like a blooming blue flower in
the night,
My love for horses is bigger than the biggest fence,
My eyes twinkle like a light green spring leaf,
When you see the spring sun it will be a relief.

My hair is as bright as the yellow sun,
My fists tighten when I'm frustrated,
My head moving to the beat,
It is a real treat.

I like dog walking more than I can put into words,
Every morning I can hear the birds,
When I'm swimming I'm like a shark,
Swiftly gliding through the water.

My anger is like a red fire,
When things rush to my head,
But it's better when I'm surrounded by family
instead,
My family is my rock,
My family makes me feel like I belong.

Hattie Partington (11)
Old Hutton CE Primary School, Old Hutton

This Is Me

When I am angry, I go a deep purple,
And I cry my heart out like Moaning Myrtle,
Then I draw a big circle,
And sit in it and grow like a turtle.

When I am sleepy I go white,
I am happy when Mummy says goodnight,
And try to go to sleep with all my might,
But soon I will be quite alright.

I have legs that will never tire,
When my muscles are burning like fire,
I think someone will want my legs to be on hire,
So they can call themselves a buyer.

My eyes water when pollen is in the air,
Coming from the field over there,
I think there is pollen in my hair;
So I am now in despair.

My brain works like a calculator,
It gives you an answer like an alligator,

My brain is a maths applicator,
When I get a question wrong, my eyes turn into
evaporators.

My love for gardening is as big as the tallest tree in
the world,
But sometimes my beautiful, green plants get
curled,
And when I watered them they greened and
unfurled,
I once saw them dance when the wind swirled and
hurled.

My love for maths is as big as the length of infinite
zeros,
When I get stuck into some work out come my
heroes,
They pull me out of the work and scatter me with
Roses,
Then they give a maths genius diagnosis.

I tell people to be respectful,
Some people are very neglectful,
Some say I am absolutely dreadful,
And some will instead be helpful.

I really like mountain biking,
I also like hill hiking,
My speed is very striking,
I charge through ferns as if I am a Viking.

Jacob Cowan (11)
Old Hutton CE Primary School, Old Hutton

This Is Me

When I'm outdoors I feel free as a bird,
Though now I think back that sounds a bit weird,
My smile is as bright as a dazzling sunflower,
So I do not mind that it gives me no power,
And I love to see animals in a herd.

I love to read a fantastic book,
Although I really don't care how I look,
The people I dare are as elaborate as I am,
But one thing I truly hate is spam,
And I also love to cook.

I love to dance and also to dream,
Because they are the things that make me beam,
I like to love,
Though I wish I could fly like a dove,
And I like to eat lactose-free cream.

Jasmine Bateman (11)
Old Hutton CE Primary School, Old Hutton

This Is Me

My smile is as bright as a miniature yellow
sunflower,
Caring is my favourite superpower!
My heart beats faster when I see my family and
friends,
Especially my best friends.

My love for gaming goes up and down - like a
dolphin in the ocean,
It makes quite a commotion!
Did you know my favourite animal is a turtle?
My passion for the world is immortal.

My love for maths is like an infinite amount of
zeros,
In my life I've seen a lot and met many heroes,
I have ears that don't plug in,
Did you know I am a twin?

My cheeks are as pink as a rose,
I don't like to pose,
I love sports,
I normally wear shorts.

I have hands that always offer kindness and care,
I'm always fair,
My love for gaming is larger than the stars,
I have fallen a lot so I have a lot of scars.

I hoped you liked reading all about me,
I have a lot of fun as you can see,
You see there are a lot of skills I employ,
They bring me a lot of joy.

Ava Sophia Natlacen (10)
Old Hutton CE Primary School, Old Hutton

This Is Me

I am as happy and as bright as a shining star,
Going far, luminous and giving light,
Sunny yellow, never mellow;
Brightening up the gloomy world around me.

I love books and I find them in nooks,
I find them exciting and read on their paper,
Whilst I caper through their adventures,
And find characters' intentions.

Have you met Harry Potter?
He went to lake bottom.
To find his best friend enchanted,
And never took him for granted again.

I have a love for sport that I cannot describe,
I'm always in the sporty vibe
And strive for glory, it's never gory;
I love running a thing that I love so much I get a bit hot,
The numbers of ruined shoes that I've got.

I love mountain biking but not hill hiking,
I've got an ace bike and I'm never on strike,
And I love forest trails and all of their details,
The ones full of hills need a lot of skills.

Florence Bateman (11)
Old Hutton CE Primary School, Old Hutton

This Is Me

In the dark and light I shine bright,
I glow like a lantern every night,
I am bold and brilliant; no matter what,
So make me sad, I think not,
I'm the light at the end of the tunnel.

My love for my horse is as large as the world,
Everything feels better when he is around; he's a
real joy,
As though he was my guardian,
He is my heart and soul,
He is my life.

My brain so tame,
Like Hermione Granger,
I may even be brainier,
I am intelligent, elegant,
And whole-hearted.

I'm clever, creative and kind,
Yes, that is me,
Thoughtful, helpful,
Original,
Me!

Eleanor Daisy Wilkinson (10)
Old Hutton CE Primary School, Old Hutton

This Is Me!

My favourite colour is ocean blue.
My bike is flashy green and black.
My legs feel strong and heavy when I go uphill.
My heart is pumping blood into my veins when I go uphill.
My hands never stop fidgeting.
I like playing on my Xbox and going on Fortnite and getting victory crowns and winning with them.
I am enthusiastic and over the top, hog wild and bonkers!
I am creative, puzzled, sporty and hysterical.
I am unique and I am the original fidgeter in Class Four.
I am a crackers special!
I am comical, fascinated by Xboxes and a nutty, cheeky chappy!

Tyson Bri Harvey (10)
Old Hutton CE Primary School, Old Hutton

This Is Me

My anger is burning red,
Emotions that help my head,
When I get to play with my friends,
I am as happy as anything,
And when I get into bed,
Not a soul can wake me up.

My family is like gold,
What is gold and is fun to play with,
My family can change me for raining tears,
Into the most contented person alive!

When I am on my Xbox I am infinitely happy,
This is because all my friends support me,
And I can enjoy myself,
Do you think that I am happy?
I think that I am.

Jake Berry (11)
Old Hutton CE Primary School, Old Hutton

This Is Me

My smile is like a bright yellow flower,
My kicks have a lot of power!
My feet run for infinity,
Sometimes I think I'm in a different reality.

I am clever,
I can write forever,
I am smart,
And I can complete my work as fast as throwing a
dart.

I am good at sports,
I like wearing shorts,
I like to play football,
I am really tall.

I like art,
I always make a good start,
I like gaming,
I am always aiming.

Owen Gravell (11)
Old Hutton CE Primary School, Old Hutton

This Is Me!

Funny, bunny bouncing for adventure.
Popping, hopping happily.
Entertaining empathic is me.
Impeccable manners is me too.

Smart but silly, clever and kind.
Hard-working, helpful but never passing down
danger.
I am an intelligent imp.
I am also a silly sausage!

My art is my life. It brings me joy when I need to
relax.
When I make art on Monday I am like Monet.
Painting, drawing, I don't care.
Give me a canvas to paint and share.

Ethan Mansfield (10)
Old Hutton CE Primary School, Old Hutton

This Is Me!

My anger is as red as the fire-burning sun,
My anger is as red as my heart.
The sky blue colour of Man City makes my heart
beat every second,
The amazing sky that's beautiful blue, but what
else is there to do?
The colour gold represents my loving, gifting
family,
I love them as much as anything in the world, more
than money and gold.
The colour black represents a flaming black hole.
The amazing, yellow, burning sun blinds my eyes
every time I look at it.

Elliott Oliver Natlacen (10)

Old Hutton CE Primary School, Old Hutton

This Is Me!

Let me free,
I want to get gaming,
That's what I am aiming.

I am funny,
Like a bunny,
I love honey and money.

I sleep,
But I don't count sheep,
I hate their bleat.

My anger is a metallic red,
When I don't want to go to bed,
But I get a sore head.

Arms that never tire;
Unlike fire,
Now I'm higher.

Lucas Robinson (11)
Old Hutton CE Primary School, Old Hutton

This Is Me

T his is me, big, brave as a lion and a good drawer.

H orses are my favourite animals, I like their manes.

I love running and jogging because that's my hobby.

S yrup on pancakes is my favourite, it is as delicious as chocolate.

I dislike having showers because soap goes in my eyes.

S mall and big siblings that are as annoying as flies and I all love.

M y dream is to go to Dubai and be a surgeon.

E ven my mum wants to go to Dubai, it's a great holiday place.

Shakar Hassan (10)
Temple Learning Academy, Halton Moor

This Is Me

T alking with my sister every night.

H aving a lot of artwork, people say I'm really good.

I love watching movies, then I sleep as tired as a sloth.

S aw Spider-Man: No Way Home twice and loved it.

I love my amazing, kind family.

S eeing my friends at school, we always have fun.

M y birthday is in February before January, as the weather gets better.

E very day of my life I'm smiling.

This is me.
I am Avie.

Avie King (9)
Temple Learning Academy, Halton Moor

This Is Me

T ravelling to brilliant Brazil to the astonishing Amazon is what I want to do.

H ave a cuddly cat and a delightful dog.

I went on the Polar Express and met Santa and Elsa.

S aving my money and being good.

I went to Scarborough.

S inging in my head at home.

M eeting new friends and playing.

E ating my favourite food and having fun.

This is me.
I am Harper.

Harper-Leigh Ellis (9)
Temple Learning Academy, Halton Moor

This Is Me

T his is my lovely life.
H ard-working, marvellous, majestic woman.
I love chunky chocolate on a rainy day.
S ometimes I can be as crazy as a clown.

I hope I become a police officer.
S ometimes I like to bake cool cakes.

M y hero is my brother when he helps people, as kind as a nurse.
E asy education is amazing.

This is me.
I am Nevaeh De Groot.

Nevaeh De Groot (10)
Temple Learning Academy, Halton Moor

This Is Me

T iny in size, as small as a mouse.
H appy Harriet and Nevaeh are my BFFs, they are as kind as a nurse.
I ntelligent nine-year-old girl.
S illy Spud is my cat.

I love my fabulous family really badly.
S pud sleeps anywhere.

M y hero is my great grandad.
E asy education is the best, I love to learn.

This is me, I am Alana Fleming.

Alana Fleming (9)
Temple Learning Academy, Halton Moor

This Is Me

T ony Hawk, my fantastic heroic hero
H e's an amazing skateboarder
I love the idea of being an archaeologist
S mart as a scientist, my pleased parents tell me.

I love to do superb swimming lessons
S wift on my feet.

M y friendly friends are spectacular and amazing to me
E ager to learn new stuff.

This is me, I am Edward.

Edward Dean (9)
Temple Learning Academy, Halton Moor

This Is Me!

T errific, yummy chocolate cake
H orrific, horrible spicy jalapeno
I like amazing, beautiful old cars
S uper maths and science.

I love my astonishing, kind family
S chool is fun.

M y brother is very funny
E xciting, terrifying speed boats, as fast as a
cheetah, on big waves are fun.

This is me
I am Seb Walker.

Seb Walker (9)

Temple Learning Academy, Halton Moor

This Is Me!

T he terrible teacher
H aunting my dreams
I gnorant teacher bossing me around
S caring me all the time.

I diotic teacher, I hope you go away
S top scaring me like a ghost.

M ean teacher go away
E xcellent teacher come.

Finally, she's here, everyone cheer.
This is me.
I am Erikson.

Erikson Camara (9)

Temple Learning Academy, Halton Moor

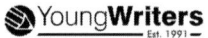

This Is Me

I'm sometimes happy
But I can be sad like a baby elephant when it cries
I'm beautiful but not always in the morning
I can look like a monkey was searching for a
banana in my hair!
I am rarely careful but often clumsy
I'm usually smart, strong, but I can't be it all the
time
I laugh when my family or friend, like Daniel, tell a
joke.
This is me!

Shelley Wood (8)
Temple Learning Academy, Halton Moor

This Is Me!

T ommy is my friend's name.
H i my name is Marcel if I didn't say.
I love football and gymnastics.
S our lemon is my favourite in water.

I like the football team Juventus.
S our Haribos are the best.

M y personality is calm.
E agles are my second best animal.

Marcel Dean (8)
Temple Learning Academy, Halton Moor

This Is Me!

T homas is my first name
H opkins is my surname name
I love football and Ronaldo and his jump
S ometimes I am sad.

I like drifting games
S econd name is Paul

M y best friends are Radu, Harry and Tommy
E ggs are disgusting.

Thomas Paul Hopkins (8)
Temple Learning Academy, Halton Moor

This Is Me!

T iny in my size.

H ave a sport.

I love rugby.

S easide is my second favourite.

I love my mum and dad and Reggie.

S carlett is my name.

M y house is big and tall and fun.

E ggs are not my favourite food!

Scarlett Burgess-Hall (7)

Temple Learning Academy, Halton Moor

This Is Me

T homas is my friend's name
H arry is my name
I live in Leeds
S am is my dad's name.

I love wildlife
S easide is the best.

M y dog's name is Bella
E lephants are my favourite animal.

Harry Keeligan-Wright (8)
Temple Learning Academy, Halton Moor

This Is Me!

T ea is good.
H ot chocolate is my favourite.
I love to eat KFC!
S ports is healthy for you.

I love to sing.
S ilence is not my thing.

M y favourite sport is dancing.
E melia is my name.

Emelia Barton (8)
Temple Learning Academy, Halton Moor

This Is Me!

T his is my poem
H i I am Lois
I am very tall for my age
S ometimes I am very sad.

I am kind and beautiful
S o is my family.

M y body is very flexible
E xcellent is what people call me.

Lois Gyimah (8)
Temple Learning Academy, Halton Moor

This Is Me

T homas is my friend's name
H arry is my friend's name
I love my family
S teler is my dog.

I love learning
S tanly is my dog.

M y name is Maison
E ggs have protein.

Maison Brady (8)
Temple Learning Academy, Halton Moor

This Is Me

I'm strong like a gorilla
But I rarely weep
I'm stressless
But sometimes I worry
I'm unique
But often normal like others
I'm happy like the sun
But often sad like a raincloud
I'm usually fun and rarely boring.

Lobopo Nkala (8)
Temple Learning Academy, Halton Moor

This Is Me

I'm strong like the crust of the Earth
I'm unique but sometimes normal
I am imperfect like a blobfish
I'm cunning like a fox
I am odd
I am fun
I am smart and that's always who I'm meant to be

This is me!

Sylvia Golonka (8)
Temple Learning Academy, Halton Moor

This Is Me

I'm cheeky like a monkey
But not always silly
I'm always intelligent
And often strong
I'm sometimes odd
But I'm amazing
I'm peaceful and always kind
I'm handsome and brave
This is me!

Joel Spenceley (7)
Temple Learning Academy, Halton Moor

My Happy Place

R eading brings me joy and comfort when I need it

E ach and every story leads to lots of adventures

A dventures that make me feel like part of the story

D uring the evening, when the rain hits the window, there's nothing better than snuggling with a book

I magining all of the characters coming to life

N othing can stop me from reading a good book

G etting lost in the stories is most of the fun.

B ig books make my imagination run wild

O ne by one I read lots of books

O ver and over getting lost in the plots

K nowing the book is almost done makes me want to read more

S o many books to get through, however, am I going to do it all?

Tilly Jones (9)
The Pilgrim School, Borstal

The Life Of Delightful Daniel

A boy

B y the kindness of his heart

C omes to be by the name of

D aniel

E very day practising piano will make his

F uture come true, he is

G ood at football and Lego

H ope for his dream will never stop

I love reading

J oy and adventure fill his veins, he

K eeps calm as a lion

L ove for his family keeps him happy

M ay his courage never be defeated, he

N ever gives up, his dream is to go to

O xford University

P erseverance helps him, he is

Q uick and speedy at homework

R eading is my favourite thing

S mart and funny

T op Gear is one of my favourite books
U nited by his family
V ery caring for others
W herever he is
X ie is my mom's surname
Y ellow is my favourite colour
Z ip it, lock it, put it in your pocket.

Daniel Wang (9)

The Pilgrim School, Borstal

This Is Me

Hello, my name is Archie,
And I like to be adventurous,
Because you get to see or find new places,
You can also climb a mountain.
I also like spending time with my friends and
family.
When I'm out in the snow, I like it
Because you can do all sorts in snow.
Like build a snowman,
Have a snowball fight
And you can go sleighing.
The foods that I love are McDonald's and Maoams
Because they're just so yummy.
Every weekday I go to The Pilgrim School and have
some fun there,
After school I go Jiu-Jitsu which is somewhere,
Where you fight people.
I like to go swimming because it's very fun
And you get to play in the pool.
The thing I like is also the Titanic,
Xbox and dinosaurs especially the velociraptor.

When I'm in the car I look outside the window
And look for cool cars and cool motorbikes,
Sometimes I see cool cars and motorbikes
But sometimes I don't.

Archie Haviland (9)
The Pilgrim School, Borstal

Happy Me!

My name is Honami and it comes from Japan,
I like cute anime girls and I'm a Pokémon fan.
My dad is Punjabi and my mum English,
Bibi Ji's pakoras are my favourite dish.

My family is Mum, Dad, Noush and my pup Rajah,
They always create a lot of drama!
We've been through a lot all together,
That means family *is* forever!

Purple is my favourite colour,
But beige is a big crusher.
Black and green are the best colours on me,
But I might look just like a tree.

I have brown eyes and long brown hair,
And so I look like a pretty mare.
I mostly wear black and funny socks,
But Mum gives my funny socks some good knocks.

My hobbies are to dance and to sing,
Making music and doing crafting.
My dreams are to go to Japan and Hawaii,
But definitely not on fish and chips Friday!

Honami Ghuman (9)
The Pilgrim School, Borstal

The Things That I Love And The Things That I Dream

I have a passion, it is football,
It makes my worries go away.
When I'm on the pitch my heart is content,
I block out the crowd and I just play.

My best friend is called Isaac,
We go everywhere together,
And along with my twin brother Harvey,
We'll be best friends forever.

Benny is my little brother,
He has crazy, curly hair.
He gives me soft, snuggly cuddles,
And he's got a snowy, white teddy called Bear.

One day I will have an English Bull Terrier,
'Snipe' will be his name.
We'll have long walks in the park,
And fetch will be his favourite game.

There's nothing I'd change in my life,
It's as exciting as can be.
These are the things that I love and I dream,
This is the poem that's all about me.

Jasper Bassett (9)
The Pilgrim School, Borstal

This Is Me

I am always busy being me,
Without it I wouldn't feel free,
I am caring and kind,
And always have a working mind.

At school I love English, art and DT,
And don't forget maths and PE,
My wonderful friends I see at school,
As a friend I love them all.

All my extra activities,
Can sometimes take over me,
But they are all so very fun,
Like dancing, scouts, swimming, hockey and ping
pong,
My love for these is still so strong.

My family who I love so very much,
Always cheer me up when I am in a grudge,
They help me out and we have some fun,
I really love my dad and mum.

This is me with a working, active mind,
With friends who are super kind,
But the subjects that I love so much,
Could never beat my dad and mum.

Ailsa Kember (10)
The Pilgrim School, Borstal

This Is Me

Hello my name is Maggie
And my mum calls me the dog trainer,
I love dogs, they're my spirit animal.

Apples are my second best food.

I'd love to get another dog,
It would be the best thing ever,
I love my dog Rudy,
Although he can be a bit of a pest.

Ellie is my big sister
And I love her but she is very annoying.

I love painting, it's just my thing.

My name is Maggie, I'm brave and I'm clever,
My mum says I'm the best dog trainer ever.
I enjoy nothing more than training my dog Rudy,
The saddest bit is when the day ends.

Maybe you'll hear me sing 'My Lighthouse',
It's my favourite hymn.

Maggie Goodwin (7)
The Pilgrim School, Borstal

Cake Of Me

Let's make a cake, a cake of me,
The ingredients will be nice, you will see.
First, add 310 kilograms of love,
That seems like a lot,
But next we need to crack open an egg of Lego stuff,
Now we add sixty-nine grams of Kirbo now,
This is looking even nicer.
Okay, let's go turbo,
Now add caster sugar of Mario,
Now put in brown sugar of FNAF,
Now this list is as long as a giraffe's neck,
Now let's get some sprinkles of joy and other games,
But we don't have time for these,
Otherwise if we did you'd get annoyed,
Finally, we need some icing of art
And some bounciness of me,
Now we've finished the cake, let's see...
It's perfect!

Dexter Maskell (10)
The Pilgrim School, Borstal

YoungWriters Est. 1991

This Is Me!

I'm Alex, I love Batman and superheroes
I love toys and boys
I love eating chocolate
I love to play Sonic Mania, Mario Kart, the Batman game and Minecraft
On my Chrome book, I really like it when it is night
I've got eyes as green as grass
I've got a brother and sister, we are all friends
I love lizards so much, I love playing with Ben and Logan.
I love the garden and I got a pirate ship and a swing and a trampoline for Christmas
From zero I turned to seven
I love watching movies and eating popcorn, I'm really smart and clever
Love going on trains to go to the museum
I love seeing my mummy and daddy
I got a Batman suit, it's terrific and cool.

Alex Scrace (7)
The Pilgrim School, Borstal

This Is Me

Samuel is my name and playing rugby is my game.
My favourite player is Owen and when I grow up I
want to be the same.
My favourite bands are Foo Fighters, White Lies,
Metallica and Queen
And to become a famous pianist is my dream.
I like gaming, I play Minecraft and FIFA 10.
One day I'd like to be as good at them as DanTDM.
My favourite films are Harry Potter and Star Wars.
Next I want to watch the Bonds, but my parents
won't let me because they are such bores.
Koalas are by far my favourite animals in the
world, they are so cute and fluffy.
I'd love to have one as a pet, but to do so I'd have
to become an Aussie.

Samuel Hockey (9)
The Pilgrim School, Borstal

Identical To Me!

I'm considerate and kind,
With a calculated working mind,
Maths is my superpower,
But English has always been my cower.

When I jump and when I run,
I realise it's so much fun,
My heart needs lots of exercise,
It pumps when I swimercise.

I'm sweet or sour,
Depending on the hour,
I'm always loud,
But whatever I do, I'm never proud.

Most of my days are full of excitement
And if I pass you I'm sure it's with a smile,
But on other days I may get mad
But usually just for a while.

This is me!
Sometimes sad with days that are bad,
But always with a smile,
Even doing the Pilgrim mile.

Lacie Phillips (11)
The Pilgrim School, Borstal

Lana, That's My Name

Hello, my name is Lana
But you can call me Lana banana.
I would like to work at a zoo,
Or maybe a chef to make yummy food.
I love Mummy's cake.
Especially her chocolate cheesecake!
I have a pet dog and his name is Kai
And when we are not home he will always cry,
But when we come home, he will jump to the sky!
When we go to the forest with Dad,
He acts as our guide, so we never need a map.
I do love mushroom hunting,
But eating them is disgusting!
At home we have lots of mugs
And the only answer there is... Mum.
Well there you go, that's my life,
And not all of these things I like.

Lana Moran (8)
The Pilgrim School, Borstal

The Ocean Life

T he ocean is full of sharks.

H arold my dog found it in the dark.

E ager to reel the abnormal eels.

O ceanic fish always tend to flourish.

C orals that are red don't really diminish.

E ven if a drop of blood comes, the ocean becomes reddish.

A normal fish can have some fluid.

N o squid has intended to be frigid.

L ion's mane jellyfish can contain some liquid.

I don't know about you but don't listen to his bid.

F orever we see there will be no acid.

E ven though it's seeable you better close your eyelids.

Donald Bakare (10)
The Pilgrim School, Borstal

Matilda And Hollie

M atilda is my name,
A lways with Hollie and Jack,
T illy for short,
I sla is the first person I met in school,
L ucia is my annoying sister,
D ad always biking around the place,
A lways playing basketball at lunch.

A lex B and Ralph doing experiments with me,
N ever giving up,
D oing dance.

H owever, I like basketball,
O lives are my favourite fruit to eat,
L ikes chemistry,
L etting people join my game,
I t's always fun to be around Hollie,
E verywhere we go we are together.

Matilda Sverha (8)
The Pilgrim School, Borstal

A Lot About Me

C PFC is my very best team,
R ed and blue, through and through!
Y ou can see me sometimes
S itting in the roaring crowd at Selhurst Park.
T hey are better than Brighton!
A t weekends I play for Rochester FC,
"L eft foot!" my dad shouts to me.

P ancakes are one of my favourite foods.
A special place to me is Kingsdown,
L eaping on the silver rocks on the stony beach
A lways makes me happy.
C onnecting letters on the Scrabble board, I
    always beat my family!
E ach of these things tells you a lot about me!

Harvey Bassett (9)
The Pilgrim School, Borstal

Johnny's Joyful Adventure Of Life And Hobbies

J oyful daffodils and dandelions dancing in the breeze are my favourite flower.

O de to Joy is a song I play on the perfect pitched piano.

H orse riding is my hobby and when I ride, I ride wildly.

N eed crunchy Cadbury chocolate, brightens up my days.

A mazing ADT is my preferred alarm box type.

'T he Diary of a Wimpy Kid' is the book I read in my dazzling room.

H appiness is Volvic which is as bubbly as sea foam.

A C/DC, I rock out to in my bright blue bedroom.

N othing better than a bit of superb Scratch and perfect Python because I code like a chimp!

Johnny Chatwell (11)
The Pilgrim School, Borstal

This Is Me!

25th August 2011 - *best day ever!*
Mum's home-made chocolate birthday cake is the best,
Friends and family come around to share this special day,
Zoom happy birthday songs from Northern Ireland,
McDonald's and orange Fanta fill my tummy,
Playing FIFA 22, feeling I am in the game,
Kylian Mbappé I become,
Bubbly Aeros like a bubble bath,
Argentina, Tenerife, Northern Ireland are where my heart is,
Dream driving my green Lamborghini,
Turquoise, the taste of the sea,
Lying on the beach feeling a big breeze,
My mind hula-hooping of dreams next year.

Jude Simmons (10)
The Pilgrim School, Borstal

My Name Is Ben

My name is Ben.
I'm cool depending on my power.
My mum doesn't like Minecraft because of her anger.
My dog turns people crazy when he chews things - he's got power.
Brussels sprouts drive me crazy.
I'm strong.
I don't like baked beans because it makes me pop.
My dog goes crazy when he doesn't go on walks.
My mum's got a love for pickled onions and my uncle loves video games.
He met my aunt at a Wimpy restaurant.
My iPad is cool.
My pants are stripy.
There's nothing more fun than playing with friends but the sad part is when it ends.

Ben Friel (7)
The Pilgrim School, Borstal

Me, And Only Me

I'm not tall, in fact I'm rather small,

I'm not big, some say I'm a bit of a twig.

My hair isn't long, it's actually short and blonde.

Although frogs are cute, I prefer horses and dogs.

Singing isn't really my thing, instead I like dancing.

I'm not the type who groans, and everyone knows my obsession with gemstones!

I can be loud and exclaiming, especially when I'm gaming.

And I love my friends and family very much, this is what I'm proclaiming.

This is me, whether you like it or not,

And being me is something I'm never going to stop.

Beatrice Nunn (11)

The Pilgrim School, Borstal

Things That I Love Doing

I love my family
S wimming is so much fun
O n Saturday I like going to rugby
B arbecues are lots of fun
E very morning I like to sleep in
L aughing with my friends I love the most
L ife is beautiful when you stop and pause
E mma is my auntie, she's so much fun.

B irthdays are the best
U nicorns are cool
T he Simpsons is the best TV show *ever!*
L ove is the best feeling of all
E gg and soldiers are really yummy
R ainy days are movie days.

Isobelle Butler (10)
The Pilgrim School, Borstal

The Hula Hooper

When I hula hoop I feel happy and joyful.
The hula hoop goes round and round
Like a roundabout at the park
Or like wheels of a car.
When I hula hoop I like to go fast on my hips
But on my legs I like to go extra fast.
It goes round and round and round and round.
I feel excited when I hula hoop
And have fun with my friends.
We hula hoop every playtime
I can jump when I am doing it
And can stand on one leg
When it goes round and round and round and round.
When it hits the floor I do it again
It makes me feel really happy.

Sienna Walker (8)
The Pilgrim School, Borstal

Me!

T rustful (you can always trust me with anything and I will keep any promise)

H onest (I never lie I'm always honest to anyone)

I mpressive (I can do lots of tricks and I can do tricks with my tongue)

S weet (I'm very kind and sweet according to my friends)

I 'm a great role model and I always do the right thing.

S uper shy (I'm quite shy but when I get to know you I become less shy)

M agical (My personality is magical!)

E nergetic (I'm quite energetic and really hyper).

Harshdeep Kaur (10)
The Pilgrim School, Borstal

This Is Me

A ll I love to do is be with family and friends,

L ove my family, they make me happy when I am down.

L ove to feed animals, my favourite are dogs.

A ll I do is play video games with my friends,

B ecause I love to walk, I am really fit,

O n special occasions, my brother is really nice at home,

U nderstandably I love everything,

T rampolining is really fun with people.

M e and my mum love to do dog walking,

E ver since I was a toddler, I have appreciated everything.

Will Tingley (10)
The Pilgrim School, Borstal

Mabel

M y name is Mabel, I am positive, adventurous and kind, breaking any rules would blow my mind.

A lthough I lost my hearing when I was young, I do not let it get in the way of having fun.

B est of all is going to school, playing with my friends and making them laugh, and having cuddles with 'Rabbi' who is not a giraffe!

E motions are my thing and my colour would be a rainbow, that has a beautiful yellow glow.

L ife's ambition is to be kind, happy and healthy, although I wouldn't mind being successful and wealthy.

Mabel Gisby (8)

The Pilgrim School, Borstal

Olivia's Trivia

O reos ice cream is the best.
L aughing with my friends.
I sobelle is my sister,
V ictor is my grandpops.
I like watching movies with my mummy and daddy and Isobelle.
A t weekends we get to stay up later.

B ut Sunday nights are early nights.
U nicorns are my favourite mythical creature.
T rampolining is fun when you do it at the funfair.
L aughing and dancing with my friends I enjoy.
E very day I like to sing.
R ock climbing is really fun.

Olivia Butler (8)
The Pilgrim School, Borstal

This Is Me!

Alex is my name, I am eight and I am old and not very fast.

I don't mind though, I wear glasses and I like winter.

I struggle with some games but my mummy believes in me.

I love space, science and geography.

For my name add a 'B' or call me 'Alexander Bradley'.

I said that before I went into Year 3 the first time.

I am quite fond of Lego and I am apart from most people wearing a black fleece.

I like space rockets and I wish to explore every planet across the bright stars they orbit.

May I be Alexander Bradley.

Alexander Bradley (8)

The Pilgrim School, Borstal

I Am Alex

I am Alex,
And I'm proud of it,
But sometimes I get angry but only for a bit.

Minecraft is my favourite game to play,
I wish I could play it every single day.

Star Wars is my sort of thing,
It just gives me this sort of bling.

Me and my sister both try our best,
But sometimes we get in a bit of a mess.

My eyes are as green as the jungle,
And when I'm in bed I get up in a bundle.

I am Alex,
And I'm proud of it,
But sometimes I get angry but only for a bit.

Alexander Swain (8)
The Pilgrim School, Borstal

The Dislikes And Likes

My favourite sport is rugby
And I don't like people saying I'm ugly
I like when my teacher says I'm very smart
But I don't like art
So really I would prefer to throw a dart
Than do art
And guess what?
No one likes a PlayStation except me
Do you see?
If you're wondering what's the most boring thing to look at is
Well for me it is a cat, a rat
And also, also some spoons and balloons
Now the last thing you should know
I want to be seen
To be a rugby player is my dream.

Stuie Petty (9)
The Pilgrim School, Borstal

Things I Like

T hings I like

H ot milk (I like banana the most, and I hate cold milk)

I ce lollies (Bubblegum flavour is my favourite)

N igeria (My home country. Note there are many tribes)

G od (I'm a Yoruba girl and also I'm a Christian)

S wan (The animal I love)

I am responsible, humble and kind!

L ilac (The flower and colour I love)

I ce lollies (Ice cream type)

K itchen (I love cooking)

E urope (Where we come together).

Ini Dele-Olateju (10)
The Pilgrim School, Borstal

All About Me!

L oves my family,
U nderstands my friends,
C olombian cousins,
A nd amazing grandparents.

R uns very fast,
O n stone and on grass,
M ountain biking I love,
A s like football and table tennis,
G ood I am at both,
N atural at many things,
U nder twelve Rochester FC player,
O wns many sporting medals,
L ucky very often,
O kay is a great word, I can use it anytime, anywhere, meaning anything.

Luca Romagnuolo (10)
The Pilgrim School, Borstal

I'm Me

My name is Effie and I love art
And Arctic animals are close to my heart
I have two guinea pigs called Moon and Star
They don't go outside but my cat goes far
I like to dance and I like to wriggle
When I'm with my friends we love to giggle
I really want to save the environment
Even though it might come with harsh judgement
I love my family and friends alike
One of my favourite memories was when I learnt
to ride a bike
I enjoy animals and fruit
And to that there can be no dispute!

Effie Hockley (10)
The Pilgrim School, Borstal

My Hopes And Dreams

I am Isaac, I am strong,
I can play rugby all day long,
I am really sporty and never ever naughty!
When I look up into the sky, my pigeons are flying high,
If they ever die, I think I would want to cry.

I wish for the world to be a better place,
Where we all have something to embrace,
I put effort into everything I do,
So that my hopes and dreams can come true,
I wish the same for you.

I am going to be the best I can possibly be,
And watch a bit less TV!

Isaac Thomas (8)
The Pilgrim School, Borstal

This Is Me!

M aths is my favourite subject, I think it's the best

A fter doing homework I'll play on the Wii so I'll take you on the quest

F aking and making faces is what I like best

E veryone that plays with me normally likes maths

M ainly I love my family because they love and care for me

E verything about maths I love, I'm going to explode

R unning I need to practise but I'm good at sport

A t ballet, I do stretches and things.

Nyasha Mafemera (8)
The Pilgrim School, Borstal

Me

I like to make things and bake things.

M y life is sometimes hard but mostly the sun is up on me.

A rt is my favourite thing to do.

G reat fun is important to me.

I like to imagine things.

N ormally I am as shy as a sparrow.

A nimation sometimes makes me laugh.

T ime is my enemy on a Monday morning!

I like Friday Forest School.

O h, I love macaroni cheese!

N ice and cosy, that's the way I like it.

Amber Heydinrych (8)
The Pilgrim School, Borstal

All About Me

Turquoise is a colour that reminds me of me,
It's relaxing and calm like the deep blue sea.
Horse riding is one of my favourite things to do,
Singing, dancing and gymnastics too.
My world is family, friends and Topper,
Reading books like 'The Explorer' and 'Harry Potter'.
I love to walk in the woods with my daddy,
I love to see the squirrels, flowers and trees.
I have two sisters, we are the Jamil three,
Linked together forever with our love of Disney.

Olivia Jamil (9)
The Pilgrim School, Borstal

Me

My hair is as bright as the sun,
I smell as fresh as a daisy,
When I feel sad, McDonald's cheers me up,
But when I'm playing football I'm full up,
I am dreaming and dreaming of becoming a footballer,
One day I will be there,
My spare McDonald's in hand reminding me of young days,
The amazement of me on my PS4,
The amazement of me with my friends,
But now I am here,
Now my head's in the game and nobody's ashamed,
Me and my football days.

Billy Cary (9)
The Pilgrim School, Borstal

Olivia R

O nce a day, Google tells me a joke.

L oving my family makes me smile but sometimes I have to wait a while!

I n our school I have some friends, Maggie, Angel and Tilly don't forget!

V ans are my favourite car but last of all a painted jar!

I nterland is my favourite game that I always like to play!

A nyday I'll make you smile but if you cry I'll still make you smile!

R ayners are the family but if we hate we are not welcome.

Olivia Rayner (8)
The Pilgrim School, Borstal

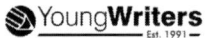

Recipe Book

I looked in my dad's old recipe book
And found a recipe with ingredients that make me!
Here are the ingredients you will see.
A mug of kindness and care,
A full cup of love for animals,
Friends and family,
A leaf of nature, one or three,
Liquids that describe me!
Here is what makes the liquids you see.
A full mug for being as brave as a lion,
Fun as a playroom and faithful as a dove.
Put it in the oven at 100°C,
Take it out and that makes me!

Scarlett Moon (9)

The Pilgrim School, Borstal

All About Me!

I love my furry, fluffy cats
I love green as bright as grass.
I am Tommy, as bright as the sun
I dream to be a famous YouTuber.
My eyes are as blue as the seawater
By the end of the day I'll be snoring away.

Me and Mr Danielson have the same birthday,
I am as fast as a lightning bolt,
I love maths more than anything in the world,
Year 3 is one of my favourite classes.

My name is Tommy and that is the best thing there can be.

Tommy Martin (7)
The Pilgrim School, Borstal

A Day In The Life Of A Gamer

Orange and red
Fun and gaming
Mabel and the table
Mason and chasing
PS and 5
Is all I need to survive
Some food, some water
A screen and a device
And add a controller
Is all I need to survive
No books,
No learning,
No reading,
Just a PS5 screen and my cats
Is all I need to survive
But mum says read
The teachers say write
But I say no,
I need to survive.

Mason Kelly (9)
The Pilgrim School, Borstal

My Name Is Moses

My name is Moses, I'm strong and I'm clever,
My mum says that I'm the best gamer ever!
I enjoy nothing more than playing with friends,
The saddest part is when the day ends.
When I'm at school, I like to do maths,
I wonder next year if I will have Miss Taffs.
My hair represents who I am and it is fun,
It grows up so tall it could reach the sun.
My name is Moses and I am just me,
And that is the very best thing I can be!

Moses Burton (8)
The Pilgrim School, Borstal

My Name Is Casey

I like dogs
I am a dog lover
I like helping, I know
I dream of games
I do most love my mum
I like playing with my little brother and playing the
Xbox, Nintendo
I dream of going to a gym when I am older
Be healthy
Be an engineer
I wanna be good at football and basketball
I love my doggies and nature swimming
I feel like being happy
Believe that if you be happy it makes a happy day
I have love for my family.

Casey Langford (9)
The Pilgrim School, Borstal

How To Make Me

To make me you will need:
A dash of kindness
Two pounds of The Pilgrim School
A few drops of happiness
A litre of brightness
One tablespoon of care for the world.

Method:
1. Add in the kindness and the car for the world in a mixing bowl and mix.
2. Slowly pour the brightness and happiness into the bowl.
3. Add in The Pilgrim School and bake in the oven for fifteen minutes.
This is how to make *me*.

Gracie Haviland (10)

The Pilgrim School, Borstal

I Love

I love football, I think it's very cool.
Football is good for your soul,
I love being in goal.
I love my sister Amyla,
We call her the smiler.
Sometimes she acts crazy,
But she is as beautiful as a daisy.
I love to play on my PS5, it is very fun,
When it's hot outside I go and play in the sun.
I love my mummy,
She has a baby in her tummy.
My dad is my best friend,
He will be until the end.

Jayden Horton-Clarke (9)
The Pilgrim School, Borstal

My Worry Gremlin

Sometimes I get a worry in my head.
It's loud and it makes me explode,
But all I know is one simple thing,
It's my Worry Gremlin.

All of what my gremlin eats is the anger inside of me.
It just loves when I do get worried and anxious.
Then it says, "Yum, it's lovely, I need this every day."

But I won't let him get in my way!
I will let it pass me each and every day.

Rylan Brown (9)
The Pilgrim School, Borstal

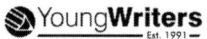

Me

L oving every day of my life
U p and down on the trampoline
C razy chemical sister soon to be Hugo's wife
I nside my dad keeps things very clean
A lways with my friends.

M aking friends and family smile
A nd the friendship never ends
R unning Pilgrim mile
I nside my heart is a place for my friends
A nother happy day being me.

Lucia Sverha (10)
The Pilgrim School, Borstal

This Is Me

L oves to see wolves and foxes.
A lways loves to go skateboarding.
U sed to hate to see blood.
G oes to the woods every now and again.
H as been playing Minecraft for three years.
T he time that I play Bloons TD 5 is only 4pm.
E very time I'm bored I love to watch YouTube.
R ough and hard things I don't like but I like soft and fluffy things.

Belle Williamson (9)
The Pilgrim School, Borstal

Faith Always Brings Happiness

F aith gives you more experience of the world.

A chievements can make you happy but not everything is will achieve.

I ndependence can be good to do.

T rustworthy is fabulous.

H ope is all we have.

F antastic people around.

U plift always and be happy when something bad happens.

L oving your family and others. Faithfulness always brings happiness.

Nafisa Hussain (10)

The Pilgrim School, Borstal

Recipe For One Autastic Felix

Take a dollop of kindness,
A dash of Minecraft,
Mash with some mods.

Mix in twenty grams of Roblox,
Add plenty of hugs,
And a sprinkling of kisses.

Stir with some YouTube,
Bake in with some autistic seasoning,
And cook for nearly eleven years.

When it's ready,
Sprinkle curls all over the top,
And you have got yourself one fantastic autastic
Felix.

Felix Barker (10)

The Pilgrim School, Borstal

Henry

H aving amazingly fun times with my fabulous friends and family.

E very day I love to learn and just become a much better person.

N ever giving up, taking any challenge head-on and trying my hardest to complete it.

R eally hard maths problems. I love maths and it is one of my favourite things.

Y ou win, you lose, but what really matters is being the best person you can be.

Henry Gardiner (10)
The Pilgrim School, Borstal

This Is Who I Am!

I like kittens
My family has a baby sister
I like Harry Potter
Black and white are my favourite colours
When it is my birthday it is Ramadan
It means no eating or drinking to teach us patience
and being calm
I like to play basketball
I wonder if I like chicken wings and chips
Fruits and roses are my favourite things
I like how Christians believe in the fruits of the
spirit.

Mariam Miah
The Pilgrim School, Borstal

This Is Me

T hey call me the Lego master,
H ere I come because I'm getting faster,
I love my cats,
S ay no presents to them because I don't like the rats.

I play football and hockey,
S ay Minecraft and I think of the world being blocky.

M arvel and Star Wars are fun to watch,
E very time I paint, it is always a big splotch.

Logan Smith (10)
The Pilgrim School, Borstal

This Is Me

My name is Jesse,
Here are some things about me,
Jack is my best friend,
At the end of the day I can get sad,
School is my favourite place to be,
It makes me happy and excited and makes me, me,
I want to protect the environment and keep it safe,
I love the seaside, it's my favourite place to be,
I love playing Super Mario,
It drives me crazy just like Haribo.

Jesse McDonagh (8)
The Pilgrim School, Borstal

This Is Me

I am a short but nice boy who lives with his pets.
I wish animals could speak, I wonder what they would say.
I love my animals so much, like the world loves me.
I am worried about overfilling the food for my fish and Milo will die.
Sometimes I am happy but sad at the same time.
I believe I give them a nice home and I have a lot that I am grateful for.
Who am I? I am Charlie

Charlie Horan (8)
The Pilgrim School, Borstal

I'm Just A Little Girl

I'm just a little girl,
I am simple and fun.
I like being with friends,
Together we're better than one.
I'm just a little girl,
I love to laugh and play.
Playing music is my thing,
I could do it all day.
I'm just a little girl,
Who has faith in God.
When I correct my actions,
He gives me a nod.
And that little girl is me.

Shontelle Gonzalo-Apolinario (10)
The Pilgrim School, Borstal

This Is Me

H ollie is my name.

O n Sunday I do lots of maths because it's my favourite subject.

L ollipops are delicious. I like to suck them and lick them.

L .O.Ls can colour change, well some can anyway.

I love to Flip Out. It's really big and fun and there is a bouncy castle.

E lsie is in my class and she loves juicy, green apples.

Hollie Atkins (8)

The Pilgrim School, Borstal

Happiness

H aving focus is really me,

A pplying knowledge every day,

P ositive attitude all the way,

P rogressing myself all day long,

I nspiring others is what I do,

N ever missing a chance to learn and grow,

E ncouraging others is how I live,

S upportive of everyone now and forever,

S o you see, this is me.

Ini Faulkner (8)
The Pilgrim School, Borstal

This Is Me

T he best is me,

H appy and joyful,

I like all the PlayStations, PS1 to PS5,

S ometimes I bake scones with my nan on Tuesdays.

I like my cute cat Lucky, he is so furry,

S onic is my favourite film.

M y mum, my dad, they are so fun,

E lephants I don't like because they are too grey.

Oscar Edwards (8)
The Pilgrim School, Borstal

Born To Dream

B elieve in yourself

O utstanding work

R eflect you words

N atural kindness

T hink before anything comes out

O btain you patience

D etermined to find out

R eveal the honesty

E ager for fun

A dore what you have

M iracles happen.

Thisana Avivalakan (10)

The Pilgrim School, Borstal

Dimitar's Snake Poem

He glides so swiftly
Back into the grass -
Gives me the courtesy of road
To let me pass,
That I am half ashamed
To seek a stone
As big as him.

S lithery as a slug
N asty as a bin
A nts have no match for him
K nowledgeable to eat its prey
E normous like the sun.

Dimitar Arabadzhiev (10)
The Pilgrim School, Borstal

Part Of Me

This is me, Zachary,
I love rugby,
I also hate tea,
This is a part of me.

I love going to the skate park with my family,
Fantastically I do a 360,
This is a part of me.

I am an outdoorsy person,
As crazy as can be,
Camping by the fire is the place for me,
This is a part of me.

Zachary Thomas (10)
The Pilgrim School, Borstal

Ralph's Poem

Without a doubt, I'm the route to get through the
long journey,
News broke out, my mum settled down,
Getting those cheese puffs out, I scoffed them
down,
The cheese all melted, I lost my money and gained
a frown.
Without a doubt, my class is more yes than no,
So I come to school for all the positives and go.

Ralph Gardiner (8)
The Pilgrim School, Borstal

Chickens - About Me

C hickens are my favourite thing.

H appy, always clucking.

I n their nice and warm house.

C aring for each other.

K ind and always hungry.

E verybody likes eggs, but for different reasons.

N o foxes are allowed.

S ome chickens are like me.

Max Fuller (9)

The Pilgrim School, Borstal

Match Day

M an of the match, I hope to be
A ll week long we train hopefully
T hursday nights are
C old and dark, I love football with all my
H eart.

D ay and night I think of
A ll the ways to kick the ball
Y earning to win the cup final!

Henry Harris (9)
The Pilgrim School, Borstal

This Is Who I Am!

I love being me,
It feels like I'm free,
Especially when I dance,
Or some say prance.

I love to bake,
My favourite food is cake,
Cake is sweet like me,
I hope you agree.

I love my family,
And they love me,
Together forever,
And ever with me.

Grace Gilbert (10)
The Pilgrim School, Borstal

My Funny Family

I have two sisters, Coralie and Amelie
This is me and my funny family
My mum and dad
Sometimes make me mad
Welcome to my funny family.

My super cute dog is called Crumpet
His bark is as loud as a trumpet
I had two rabbits called Bluebell and Spot
Them I never forgot.

Orla Skelton (10)
The Pilgrim School, Borstal

This Is Me

Running, tennis, basketball,
I love to do them all.
But my favourite game is football,
I think it's very cool!

I love to play video games,
Racing cars and changing lanes.

Going to school is good I think,
But playing with friends at break is what I like best!

Ireoluwa Dele-Olateju (7)
The Pilgrim School, Borstal

Friends Are The Best

F abulous and funny
R unning together on the playground
I ce cream is the best with friends
E xtremely happy times together
N ice friends are good to have
D ancing is cool when you do it together
S miling is what I do when they are around.

Evie Alexander (8)
The Pilgrim School, Borstal

This Is Who I Am

I am made up of:
Two tablespoons of kindness,
One bowl of co-operation,
A quarter tablespoon of gratitude,
Ten ounces of compassion,
Two teaspoons of humour,
One cup of thoughtfulness,
Half a cup of gentleness,
And last but not least,
Three bowls of smartness.

Riley Deards (10)
The Pilgrim School, Borstal

Penguin

P ears are my favourite greens.
E lephants are my favourite animal.
N intendo is my favourite.
G oats are my favourite.
U mbrellas help me in the rain.
I t is my favourite game to play.
N uts are not a penguin's favourite.

Angel Eliasova (9)
The Pilgrim School, Borstal

Me

T hankful for everything
H elpful when possible
I ntelligent and eager to learn
S arcastic.

I nterested in other's interests
S hort but with tall ideas.

M inecraft enthusiast
E xcellent at maths.

Bauer Packman-Fullbrook (11)

The Pilgrim School, Borstal

Making Me

A cup of amazing good looks.
One pint of pure happiness.
A dash of pickled naughtiness.
A bucket full of crazy laughter.
One teaspoon of growing anger.
A gallon of growing brains.
One spoonful of sadness.
A litre of liquid love.
Makes one Maxwell Libbeter.

Maxwell Libbeter (8)
The Pilgrim School, Borstal

All About Me!

There are lots of things you don't know about me
I love dancing, sewing and my family
I am kind and caring and I love children too
Especially Jenson who is my nephew
In dancing, I have won lots of medals and trophies
I try to glide around the floor like fairies.

Ava Cave (9)
The Pilgrim School, Borstal

To Make Me

How to make 'n' bake me!
Pour the korfball in the hoop
A splash of family
A hint of sugar mixed with love
A dash of milk for my pussycat
A lot of love for my two guinea pigs
I am a persevering, purple Pilgrim
Mix in with lots of energy!

Lucy-Rose Dodson (10)
The Pilgrim School, Borstal

This Is Me

F lip Out is my favourite place to go,
R ed roses are my favourite flower,
E lephants are my second favourite animal,
Y es to McDonald's but no to Brussels sprouts,
A nimals are so cute.

This is the best I can be.

Freya Craig (8)
The Pilgrim School, Borstal

This Is Me

D ancing is what I love, making up great shows!
A lways playing TT Rock Stars with my friends
I dream of being a butterfly floating in the sky
S nakes scare me, I don't like them
Y ellow daisies are just like me!

Daisy Feltham (8)
The Pilgrim School, Borstal

I Love Science

S ome people say

C hemistry is explosive fun

I f you make it random

E xperiments give you knowledge

N ew ideas are great

C an you think of new ideas?

E ven you can join in on the fun of science!

Phoenix Collins (10)

The Pilgrim School, Borstal

This Is Me

I love to play with my dog Jack,
I throw a ball and he brings it back.
I love to jump on a trampoline,
I can do the highest bounce you've ever seen!
I love my family, they make me smile,
I get sad when I have to leave them for a while.

Daphne Balseca (8)
The Pilgrim School, Borstal

This Is Me!

N uala is my name and I like to play

U nusually my name is Irish

A ctually I'm adventurous and have a rebellious spirit

L ove to play with Jax

A ll I do is be me, it's not hard to be the best me I can be!

Nuala Walker-Pemble (7)

The Pilgrim School, Borstal

This Is Me

Hello my name is Isla,
My mum calls me smiler.
I like to see my cousins,
I like it because I love them.
I love playing with my friends,
I can't wait for the day to end.
This is me Isla,
I love my life, it's a smiler!

Isla Thomas (8)
The Pilgrim School, Borstal

Finlay

I am Finlay.
I like spiders and sharks.
They swim fast.

I like apples too,
Also my birthday is in August.

I am fast because
I never get to school late!

I am Finlay and that is the best
I can be.

Finlay Ashby (7)
The Pilgrim School, Borstal

This Is Me

Minecraft is the best but walks are a snore-fest
Tuna meatballs make me smile but olives make me
belch out loud
I want to be the fastest being, the quickest is my
dream
I'm very, very agile, it is my favourite hobby
This is me.

Beau Hockley (8)
The Pilgrim School, Borstal

My Favourite Things To Do!

Jessie, my best friend, likes playing football with me.
Alex Swain is smart and like a calculator, he's good at maths.
Cancelling playtime is sad but they get toys out!
Cackling like an old lady when I'm eating my toffee apples.

Jack Harris (7)
The Pilgrim School, Borstal

Me

S ounds of a basketball bouncing,
P laying video games and music,
O ld, furry, energetic and cheerful,
R apid wifi on the phone,
T houghtful, happy and brave,
Y ellow button to watch anime.

Joshua Harrison (11)
The Pilgrim School, Borstal

My Everything

F ull of joy, blessing and happiness
A lways there for me
M y backup, my guidance and my wisdom
I ndescribable amounts of support
L ove in abundance
Y ou and me always and forever.

A J Hurkoo (9)
The Pilgrim School, Borstal

This Is Me

L ove the way my mum cares for me.

O bviously, I love Mr Jeff.

G reen juicy apples, I love them.

A pples covered in toffee are my favourite!

N othing I like more than playing video games.

Logan Baxter (8)

The Pilgrim School, Borstal

This Is Me

K idzone is my favourite place to go.
R eading in peace makes me calm.
I love to play about with my friends.
T elling stories to me makes me interested.
I love eating ice cream.

Kriti Arivalakan (7)

The Pilgrim School, Borstal

This Is Me

A pples are my favourite fruit, bananas I detest!
N ever angry, always kind,
G eorge Vaults is where my mum works.
E nglish is my favourite lesson,
L ove my family so very much.

Angel Darling (7)
The Pilgrim School, Borstal

My Poem

My name is Koby,
I like to play with my friends.
I like Lego too.
I dream of being an illustrator.
When I'm in school my friends are so cool.
I am Koby and this is the best thing I can be.

Koby Packman (8)
The Pilgrim School, Borstal

This Is Me!

Riley,
Smiley, creative
Brother to Jude and Eliza
Enjoys arts and crafts and riding my bike
My heart smiles when I see my friends
Protective, loving
Simmons.

Riley Simmons (7)

The Pilgrim School, Borstal

The Josh Poem

My name is Josh
I love my family
They keep me sane
And make me happy.
I play my Xbox next to my panda
I play with my friends
I like swimming with Sandra.

Joshua Sheppard (9)
The Pilgrim School, Borstal

This Is Me

Cat loving,
Dog hugging,
Colouring queen,
Swims like a dream,
Elsie's friend.

This is me!

Olivia Lawniczak (7)
The Pilgrim School, Borstal

YOUNG WRITERS INFORMATION

We hope you have enjoyed reading this book – and that you will continue to in the coming years.

If you're the parent or family member of an enthusiastic poet or story writer, do visit our website **www.youngwriters.co.uk/subscribe** and sign up to receive news, competitions, writing challenges and tips, activities and much, much more! There's lots to keep budding writers motivated!

If you would like to order further copies of this book, or any of our other titles, then please give us a call or order via your online account.

Young Writers
Remus House
Coltsfoot Drive
Peterborough
PE2 9BF
(01733) 890066
info@youngwriters.co.uk

Join in the conversation!
Tips, news, giveaways and much more!

 **YoungWritersUK**    **YoungWritersCW**    **youngwriterscw**